박노해 사진에세이

06

올리브나무아래

BENEATH
THE OLIVE
TREE

PARK NOHAE PHOTO ESSAY 06

느린걸음

언제나 그 자리에 서서
나를 기다려주고 지켜주는 나무 하나
그토록 묵중하고 한결같은 사람 하나
천 년의 올리브나무 아래

A tree that always stands there
waiting for me and protecting me.
A person who is so profound and consistent.
Beneath a thousand-year-old olive tree.

CONTENTS

Preface

My Olive Tree · 13

Photography

Morning in the olive grove · 18   The monastery in the wilderness · 22

The old man and the trees · 24   A small spring · 26   Three olive trees · 30

Under the protection of a sacred grove · 32   A Palestinian mother · 36

Laboring in the olive grove · 38   A thousand years of love · 40

The path spring takes · 42   If you run over stony ground · 46

When the Azan sounds · 48   Breakfast at Al Jazeera · 50   Daily picnic · 52

A place for the soul · 54   A woman preparing dinner · 56

A young tree in the wilderness · 58   A green belt in the occupied territories · 62

"This wall will collapse" · 64   Hope engraved on the wall of despair · 68

Thousand-year-old olive trees decapitated · 70   Refugee camp posters · 72

A thousand years begins like this · 74   The place where Jesus was born · 78

Survival amidst the bombing · 80   An olive branch on a gravestone · 82

New leaves sprout on a burnt tree · 84   The girl who grew up with trees · 88

Highland encourager · 90   Even if the cross is broken · 92   Sunset prayer · 94

Beneath an olive tree · 96   My tree · 100   Tree calls to tree · 102   Take this fruit · 104

Like a faithful watchman · 106   Holding a lamb in his arms · 108

Biography · 113

Books · 116

서문

나의 올리브나무 · 9

작품

올리브나무 숲의 아침 · 18   광야의 봉쇄수도원 · 22   노인과 나무 · 24

작은 샘물 하나가 · 26   올리브나무 세 그루 · 30   성림聖林의 가호 아래 · 32

팔레스타인의 어머니 · 36   올리브 숲의 노동 · 38   천 년의 사랑 · 40

봄이 오는 길 · 42   돌밭을 달려도 · 46   아잔 소리 울리면 · 48

알 자지라의 아침식사 · 50   날마다 소풍 · 52   영혼을 위한 자리 · 54

저녁을 준비하는 여인 · 56   사막의 어린 나무 · 58   점령지의 푸른 띠 · 62

"이 벽은 무너지리라" · 64   절망의 벽에 새긴 희망 · 68

목 잘린 천 년의 올리브나무 · 70   난민촌의 포스터 · 72

천 년의 시작은 이렇게 · 74   예수가 태어난 자리에 · 78   폭격 속에 살아남아 · 80

묘석 위의 올리브 가지 · 82   불탄 나무에 새잎이 돋다 · 84

나무와 함께 자란 소녀 · 88   고원의 격려자 · 90   십자가는 부러져도 · 92

석양의 기도 · 94   올리브나무 아래 · 96   나의 나무는 · 100

나무는 나무를 부른다 · 102   이 열매를 받으라 · 104   믿음의 파수꾼처럼 · 106

어린 양을 품에 안고 · 108

약력 · 113
저서 · 116

나의 올리브나무

분쟁 현장을 다니다, 나도 많이 다쳤다. 전쟁의 세상에서 내 안에 전쟁이 들어서려 할 때, 나는 절룩이며 천 년의 올리브나무 숲으로 간다.

푸른 올리브나무에 기대앉아 막막한 광야를 바라보며 책을 읽고 시를 쓰다가, 살았는지 죽었는지도 모를 아이들과 친구들의 얼굴이 떠올라 눈물짓다가, 올리브나무 사이를 걸으며 다윗처럼 돌팔매를 던지기도 하고, 저 아래 올리브를 수확하는 농부들을 거들다가 돌샘에서 목을 축이고, 양떼를 몰던 소녀가 따다 주는 한 움큼의 무화과를 먹고, 온 광야와 하늘을 붉게 적시는 석양에 나도 물들어가다가, 또 밤이 걸어오고 별이 돋아나면 올리브나무 아래서 기도를 드리고, 그렇게 심히 상한 몸과 마음을 소생시켜 다시 일어서곤 했다.

천 년의 올리브나무 숲은 나의 비밀한 수도원이었고 이 검푸른 지구 위에 한 점 빛의 장소였다.

그때 그곳에서 올리브나무가 이르기를, '오랜 세월 동안 나에게도 많은 일이 있었어. 그래도 살아왔어. 늘 푸른 빛을 잃지 않았어. 고난 속에서도 최선의 열매를 맺어 주었어. 천 년의 세월을 내가 기억하고 있어. 내가 지켜가고 있어. 좌절하지 말고 포기하지 말고 너의 길을 가.' 나는 젖은 눈의 소년이 되어 깊은 숨을 쉬었다.

　　나에게 올리브나무는 오래고도 한결같은 사랑 그 자체다. 척박한 땅에서 온몸을 비틀며 자신을 짜 올려, 고귀한 열매와 황금빛 기름과 사랑으로 맺어 올린 좋은 것들을 남김없이 내어주는 나무. 올리브나무가 '천 년의 사랑'으로 살아온 것은 한순간도 쉬임 없이 견뎌냈고, 강해졌고, 새로워졌기 때문이다. 상처를 통해 더 온전함으로 나아가고 시련을 통해 더 고귀함으로 빛나고자 고요하고 끈질기게 싸워왔기 때문이다. 울퉁불퉁한 나무 둥치, 찢기고 꺾여진 가지, 깊이 구멍 뚫린 심장. 올리브나무의 신성한 기운은 바로 그 사랑의 성흔聖痕에 있다. 천 년의 올리브나무를 보며 나는 다시 사랑을 배우곤 한다.

　　세상이 빠르게 변하고 있다. 아이들은 성공을 재촉당하고 어른들은 성과를 부정당하고, 시류와 유행을 따라 알려지고 인정받지 않으면 쓸모없는 존재인 양 무시당하고 있다. 난폭한 권력과 안주한 세력이 나라의 위기를 불러오고, 탐욕과 혐오와 적대와 환멸을 불지르고 있다. 어디에도 희망은 없고 누구 하나 바라볼 사람이 없고, 불안과 우울과 무력감 속에 덧없는 행복과 위락에 탐닉하고 있다. 그리하여 다들 쉽게 살려 하고 편히 가지려 하고, 각박하게 자기 앞만 바라보게 떠밀리는 사이, 세상이 다 이렇고 인간은 이런 거라고 '악의 신비'가 드리울 때면, 나는 천 년의 올리브나무를 바라본다.

　　우리는 좀 더 강인해져야 한다. 고귀한 인간 정신으로, 진정한 나 자신으로, 저 광야의 올리브나무처럼 푸르르고 강해져야 한다.

　　세상이 결코 만만하지 않은 것처럼 인간은 결코 간단한 존재가 아니다. 아무리 시대가 그래도, 우리 주변에는 생각보다 더 많이 좋은 사람들이 살아 숨 쉬고 있다. 누가 알아주지 않아도 자신이 선 자리에서 힘겹게 양심과 원칙을 지켜가는 사람들. 대가나 보상을 바라지 않고 자신이 가진 소중한 것을 기꺼이 내어주는 사람들. 시류에 휩쓸리지 않고 묵묵히 자기 할 일을 해 나가는 사람들. 누가 보아주지 않아도 좋은 삶을 살아가며 선한 메아리를 울려오는 사람들. 나에게 빛이 되고 힘이 되고 길이 되는 사람 하나 올리브나무처럼 몸을 기울여 나를 기다리고 있다.

우리 인생은 훨씬 크고 장엄하고 고귀한 것이다. 나 하나는 세계의 최소 단위이자 세계의 모든 것이기도 한 존재다. 희망의 단서端緒인 나 하나를 지켜내야 한다. 그렇게 서로를 알아보고 경외하고 함께 걸어가는 용기를 내야 할 때이다. 척박한 광야에서도 작은 올리브나무 하나가 스스로 뿌리를 내리고 살아남으면, 그러면, 나무는 나무를 부르고 숲은 숲을 부르며, 다시 천 년의 사랑이 시작된다. 이런 시대에 작은 올리브나무 같은 나 하나로부터 우리 삶을 지키는 푸른 방패가 되고 소리 없이 세상을 지탱하는 푸른 기둥이 되어갈 것이니.

여기 천 년의 '올리브나무 아래' 기대어 그대 안의 신성한 빛과 강인한 힘을 길어 올리기를. 언제나 그 자리에 서서 나를 기다려주고 지켜주는 나무 하나, 그토록 묵중하고 한결같은 사람 하나, 천 년의 올리브나무 아래.

2023년 9월
박노해

My Olive Tree

Going to the scene of battlefields, I too was badly hurt. In a world full of war, when war is about to enter me, I limp into a thousand-year-old olive grove.

After leaning against a green olive tree and looking at the vast wilderness, reading books and writing poems, remembering the faces of children and friends who might be alive or dead, shedding tears, walking among the olive trees, throwing stones like David, helping the farmers harvest the olives down there, quenching my thirst from a stone spring, eating a handful of figs picked by a girl herding sheep, and basking in the setting sun that makes the whole wilderness and sky red, then when night falls and the stars appear, I pray beneath an olive tree, restore my terribly wounded body and heart, and stand up again.

The thousand-year-old olive grove was my secret monastery and a gleam of light in this dark blue earth.

Then, there, the olive tree said, 'A lot has happened to me over many years. Yet I've survived. I've never lost my green glow. Even in the midst of hardships, I bore the best fruit. I remember the thousand years. I'm watching over everything. Don't get frustrated, don't give up, go your way.' I became a tearful boy and took a deep breath.

To me, the olive tree is a long and constant love itself. A tree that twists its body and squeezes itself on barren land, giving away noble fruits, golden oil, and all the good things it has produced through love. The reason why the olive tree has lived as a 'thousand-year love' is that it has endured without a moment's rest, ever becoming stronger, ever becoming new. It is because it has been fighting silently and persistently, advancing toward more wholeness through wounds, shining with more nobility through trials. A gnarled tree trunk, torn and broken branches, a deeply pierced heart. The divine energy of the olive tree is in the stigma of love. Looking at the thousand-year-old olive tree, I learn to love again.

The world is changing rapidly. Children are pushed to succeed, adults are denied their achievements, and are ignored as if they are useless unless they are known and recognized according to the current trends and fashions. Violent power and complacent forces are causing a crisis in every nation, stoking greed, hatred, hostility, and disillusionment. There is no hope anywhere and no one to look to, and people indulge in fleeting happiness and pleasures amid anxiety, depression, and helplessness. So, while everyone is trying to live easily and enjoy what they have, and are pushed to look only in front of themselves, when the 'mystery of evil' hangs over us, with the world like this and human beings like this, I look at the thousand-year-old olive tree.

We have to be a little tougher. With a noble human spirit, with my true self, I must become green and strong like an olive tree in the wilderness.

Just as the world is never easy, humans are never simple beings. Even if the era is not good, there are more good people living and breathing around us than we thought. People who struggle to keep their conscience and principles as they stand their ground, even if no one recognizes them. People who are willing to give away their valuables without expecting anything in return or reward. People who quietly do their job without being swept away by the current. People who live a good life and produce good echoes even when no one is watching. One person who becomes my light, strength, and path is waiting for me, leaning like an olive tree.

Our life is much bigger, more majestic and nobler. I alone am the smallest unit of the world, and also everything in the world. I have to protect myself, the clue to hope. It's time to recognize each other, be in awe of each other, and take the courage to walk together. Even in the barren wilderness, if a small olive tree takes root and survives, then tree calls to tree, forest calls to forest, and the love of a thousand years begins again. In this era, I, like a small olive tree, will become a green shield that protects our lives, and a green pillar that silently supports the world.

Leaning here 'beneath the thousand-year-old olive tree,' I hope you draw up divine light and powerful strength from within yourself. A tree that always stands there waiting for me and protecting me. A person who is so profound and consistent. Beneath a thousand-year-old olive tree.

September, 2023
Park Nohae

올리브나무 숲의 아침

고대의 정취가 어려있는 제라시에는
100만 그루 이상의 올리브나무가 자라고 있다.
인류 역사에서 가장 오래된 유실수有實樹이자
가장 오래 살아남는 나무인 올리브나무는
"나무 중의 으뜸", "우주의 기둥"으로 불려왔다.
그리스 로마 신화부터 성서, 쿠란, 일리아스, 천일야화 등
수많은 고전과 경전에도 빠지지 않고 등장하는 나무다.
붉은 광야에 푸른 올리브나무들이
태양빛을 받으며 눈부시게 현신顯身하는 아침.
천 년의 시간을 걸어와 '나 여기 서 있다'.

MORNING IN THE OLIVE GROVE

In the city of Jerash, where a feel of ancient times lingers, more than
one million olive trees grow. The oldest fruit tree in human history, and
the oldest living tree, the olive tree has been called "best of trees" and
"pillar of the universe." From Greco-Roman mythology to the Bible, the Quran,
the Iliad, the One Thousand and One Nights, and more, the olive tree appears
without fail in countless classics and sacred books. Each morning green olive
trees in a red wilderness loom dazzling in the sunlight. 'I am standing here,'
they say, having come walking through a thousand years.

Jerash, Jordan, 2008.

광야의 봉쇄 수도원

유대 광야 한가운데 자리한 마르사바 봉쇄수도원은
세계에서 가장 오래된 수도원 중 하나이다.
5세기경 광야와 동굴에서 은둔 수도 생활을 시작한
성뿔 사바를 따라 그처럼 살기 원하는 젊은이들이 모여
당시 가장 크고 높은 수도 공동체를 이루었다.
세월의 바람은 모든 걸 휩쓸어가고,
이제 이곳에는 십여 명의 수도자만이 남았다.
바람 센 언덕에서 대를 이어 자라온 작은 올리브나무는
다시 온몸으로, 자신의 시대를 살아내고 있다.

THE MONASTERY IN THE WILDERNESS

The Mar Saba Monastery is located in the heart of the Judean Wilderness.
It is one of the oldest monasteries in the world. Young men gathered there,
following and living like Saint Sabbas, who in the 5th century began to
live a secluded life as a hermit in the wilderness and in caves, and formed
the largest, the most high-minded monastic community of those days.
The winds of time have swept away everything, and now there are only about
a dozen monks left here. A small olive tree that has grown from generation
to generation on the windy hill is intently living its own era whole-heartedly.

The Wilderness East of Bethlehem, Palestine, 2005.

노인과 나무

대대로 물려받은 올리브나무 사이를 걷는 농부.
"어려서부터 할아버지 손을 잡고 아침저녁마다
이곳에서 하루를 시작하고 하루를 마쳤지요.
힘들고 괴로운 일이 있을 때면 올리브나무들이
'괜찮다 괜찮다 좋은 날이 올 거야' 저를 안아주었고
좋은 일이 있을 때면 나무 아래 감사 기도를 드리며
선조들을 기억하고 앞을 바라보곤 하지요.
그렇게 긴 세월 우리는 서로를 지켜왔지요."
붉은 석양이 물들어 오면 그는 한 그루 한 그루
올리브나무를 순례하며 하루의 생을 정리한다.

THE OLD MAN AND THE TREES

A farmer goes walking among the olive trees inherited from generation to generation. "Since I was little, holding my grandfather's hand, every morning and evening I've been starting and ending each day here. When there were hard and painful things, the olive trees would hug me, saying, 'It's okay, it's okay, good days will come.' When good things happen, I pray beneath the trees and give thanks, remembering my ancestors and looking ahead. We have been protecting each other for so long." When the red sunset shines out, he makes a pilgrimage to the olive trees, one by one, marking the end of the day.

Jerash, Jordan, 2008.

A SMALL SPRING

The water flowing ceaselessly from a small spring among the rocks in
the wilderness, together with the rain falling at the right time, forms a powerful
stream that gives birth to a miraculous landscape where the barren land
turns green. From this little spring in the burning wilderness wildflowers bloom
in green meadows, olive trees form a green path, where birds and flocks of
sheep and camels rear their young, and people live along that path.
A stream of water in the wilderness is literally water of life, a path of life.
Even today, the small spring in the wilderness flows clear water.

The Wilderness East of Bethlehem, Palestine, 2005.

작은 샘물 하나가

광야의 작은 돌샘에서 쉬임 없이 흘러나오는 물은
때가 되어 내리는 비와 함께 힘찬 물살을 이루며
메마른 땅이 푸르러지는 기적 같은 풍경을 낳는다.
불타는 광야의 이 작은 샘물로부터
푸른 초장草場에 야생화가 피어나고
올리브나무는 푸른 길을 내어가고
새들과 양떼와 낙타가 새끼를 치고
사람이 그 길을 따라 살아나간다.
광야의 물줄기는 말 그대로 생명수, 생명의 길이다.
오늘도 광야의 작은 샘은 맑은 물을 흘려보낸다.

올 리 브 나 무 세 그 루

한때는 올리브 숲이었으나, 세월이 흘렀다.
거친 바위 산에 살아남은 올리브나무 세 그루.
누가 보아주지 않아도 자신의 자리에서
단단히 뿌리를 내리고 서 있는 저 나무들은
세상을 떠받치는 기둥처럼 굳건하다.
사람은 나무와 같아서, 자신이 그런 줄도 모른 채
하나의 비밀스러운 기둥이 되어
이 세상을 지탱하고 있는 그런 사람들이 있다.

THREE OLIVE TREES

There was once an olive grove here, but years have passed.
Now just three surviving olive trees on a rough rocky mountain.
Even if no one is watching, those trees standing firmly rooted in their place,
are strong like pillars holding up the world. People being like trees,
there are people who, unaware, become secret pillars and support this world.

Jerash, Jordan, 2008.

UNDER THE PROTECTION OF
A SACRED GROVE

Salfit Village, where olive groves spread endlessly. Seen from the plateau,
the leaves change according to the sun and wind, shining dark green, bronze,
silver gray, exuding fresh vitality and enveloping us in spiritual energy.
Here, those who cultivated olive groves for generations in the old belief that
the olive tree was the center of the world, are sleeping while their descendants
live on under the protection of this sacred grove.

Salfit, Palestine, 2005.

성림聖林의 가호 아래

올리브나무 숲이 끝도 없이 펼쳐지는 살핏 마을.
고원에서 바라보면 태양과 바람에 따라 잎새들이
진녹색으로 청동색으로 은회색으로 빛나며
신선한 생기를 뿜어내고 신령한 기운에 감싸이게 한다.
올리브나무를 세상의 중심이라 여긴 오래된 믿음 아래,
여기 대대로 올리브나무 숲을 일궈온 이들이 잠들어 있고
후손들은 이 성림聖林의 가호를 받으며 살아간다.

팔 레 스 타 인 의 어 머 니

정성껏 올리브나무 가지를 손질하던 여인이
고원의 바람결에 잠시 숨을 고른다.
"우리에게 많은 일이 있었지요.
땅을 빼앗기고 길을 빼앗기고 앞을 빼앗기고,
아이들이 자라나 청년이 되면 하나 둘 죽어가고….
그런 날이면 올리브나무가 말해주곤 하지요.
오랜 세월 동안 나에게도 많은 일이 있었다고.
그래도 살아왔다고, 푸른빛을 잃지 않았다고.
고난 속에서도 최선의 열매를 맺어 주었다고.
그렇지요…. 그렇게 살아가는 거지요."
팔레스타인의 어머니는 먼 곳을 바라본다.

A PALESTINIAN MOTHER

A woman carefully pruning olive branches takes a moment to catch
her breath in the highland breeze. "We have been through a lot.
The land has been taken, the roads have been taken, the future has been taken.
When the children grow up and become young adults, they die one after another….
And on such days, the olive tree speaks to me, saying: I have been through
a lot over the years, but still, I have survived, and have not lost my blue hue,
even in the midst of hardship, I have borne my best fruit. That's right….
That's how to live." The Palestinian mother gazes into the distance.

Salfit, Palestine, 2008.

올리브 숲의 노동

마을 축제와도 같은 올리브 수확철이 되면
청년들과 노인들과 아이들까지 모두 모여
올리브 숲에서는 웃음소리 노랫소리가 울려온다.
올리브를 수확한 뒤 정리해 준 가지들은
가축의 먹이가 되고 가구가 되고 땔감이 된다.
올리브나무 숲에서 노동을 한다는 건
단순히 돈이 되는 일을 하는 것만이 아니다.
여기 태어나 지상의 한 인간으로, 역사의 전승자로,
하늘과 땅 사이 온 생명 공동체의 주체로,
나와 우리가 만나서 서로의 존재를 빛내는 일이다.

LABORING IN THE OLIVE GROVE

During the olive harvest, which is like a village festival, young people,
old people and children all gather together and in the olive groves,
the sound of laughter and singing echoes. Branches pruned after the olives
have been harvested become food for livestock, furniture, and firewood.
Working in the olive grove is not just about making money.
Born here, as a human on earth, as a successor of history,
as a member of the life community between heaven and earth,
it's a matter of I and we meeting and making each other's existence shine forth.

Salfit, Palestine, 2008.

천 년 의 사 랑

팔레스타인 광야의 천 년 된 올리브나무.
올리브나무가 천 년을 살아도 이토록
키가 크지 않는 건 사랑, 사랑 때문이다.
하루하루 온몸을 비틀며 자신을 짜 올려
사랑으로 피고 맺은 좋은 것들을 다
아낌없이 내어주고 바쳐왔기 때문이다.
보라, 구멍 나고 주름 깊은 내 모습을.
내 상처의 성흔聖痕을. 이 모습 그대로가 사랑이니.
구멍 뚫린 그 자리에 신성한 잉태의 빛을 품고
오늘도 아이 같은 새순을 밀어 올리는
천 년의 사랑, 천 년의 올리브나무.

A THOUSAND YEARS OF LOVE

A thousand-year-old olive tree in the wilderness of Palestine.
The reason an olive tree is not very tall even if it lives a thousand years,
is because of love, love. It is because it has twisted its body day by day
and squeezed itself, as it has generously given, dedicated to
all the good things that have bloomed and ripened out of love.
See me with my holes and deep wrinkles, the stigmata of my wounds.
Love looks like this. Embracing the light of divine conception
where the holes are, today, it is pushing up new shoots like children,
a thousand years of love, a thousand years of olive tree.

Salfit, Palestine, 2005.

THE PATH SPRING TAKES

Borne by the Tigris and Euphrates rivers, spring has returned to
the Al Jazeera plains. Light green wheat sprouts on the dark red earth,
the olive trees put out flower buds, a herd of sheep leisurely passes by
on a curved hill road. Farmers, shepherds, lambs, and olive trees, each with
a sincere, gentle and persistent gait, does its own thing, goes its own way.
Brilliant stillness, morning of rebirth. Spring is here! Spring!

Tell Mardikh, Syria, 2008.

봄이 오는 길

티그리스 강과 유프라테스 강이 밀어 올린
알 자지라 평원에 다시 봄이 찾아왔다.
검붉은 대지에 연초록 밀싹이 돋아나고
올리브나무는 꽃눈을 틔워내고
둥근 언덕길로 유유히 양떼가 지나간다.
농부들도 목동들도 어린 양도 올리브나무도
성실하고 부드럽고 끈질긴 걸음으로
자신의 일을 하고 자신의 길을 간다.
눈부신 고요, 신생의 아침, 봄이다 봄!

돌밭을 달려도

메말랐던 광야에 봄비가 내리면
온 대지가 하루아침에 싱싱하게 살아난다.
양떼에게 새 풀을 먹이던 아이들은
공 하나만 있으면 신나게 뛰어논다.
돌밭을 달려도, 돌길에 채여도,
부딪히고 넘어지고 상처가 좀 나도,
공처럼 둥근 마음으로 통통 튀어 오른다.
등 뒤에 있는 올리브나무는 아이들의 수호자.
'네 뒤에는 우리가 있어, 마음껏 뛰놀고 꿈을 꿔.
울고 웃고 함께 앞을 바라보며 너만의 길을 가.'

IF YOU RUN OVER STONY GROUND

When the spring rain falls in the barren wilderness the whole land
comes to life afresh overnight. The children feeding the sheep with new grass,
if they have only one ball, can run happily. Even if they run over stony ground,
even if they get knocked by the stony road, even if they bump into each other
and fall and get hurt, they come bouncing back up with hearts round like a ball.
The olive tree behind them is the children's guardian.
'We are behind you, so run around and dream to your heart's content.
Cry, laugh, look forward together, and go your own way.'

Jerash, Jordan, 2008.

아 잔 소 리 울 리 면

중동의 광야에는 날카로운 분쟁의 폭음과
고요하고 신성한 음률音律이 함께 흐른다.
그래도, 올리브나무 새싹은 다시 피어나고
갓 태어난 어린 양의 울음소리가 들려오고
연인들이 수줍은 떨림으로 입맞춤을 하고
석양의 아잔 소리가 길게 울리면,
삶은 그대로 살람Salam, 평화이다.

WHEN THE AZAN SOUNDS

In the wilderness of the Middle East the explosion of sharp strife,
and quiet, sacred melodies flow together. Still, the olive trees bud again,
the cry of newborn lambs is heard, lovers kiss, trembling shyly.
When the sunset Azan sounds long, life is simply Salam, peace.

Jerash, Jordan, 2008.

알 자 지 라 의 아 침 식 사

알 자지라 평원의 아침식사는 소박하나 풍요롭다.
"첫 비가 오고 첫 얼굴을 보고, 오늘은 좋은 날.
먼 데서 온 형제여, 우리 함께 빵을 나눕시다."
양젖 요구르트에 레몬즙과 후추를 뿌리고
올해 수확한 신선한 올리브기름을 두르고
자두절임과 고추피클, 허브치즈와 야생 꿀,
화덕에서 구워낸 빵과 샤이를 내어온다.
음식마다 빠짐없이 들어가는 올리브기름의
아릿하고 싱그러운 향이 입안 가득 번질 때,
올리브는 그야말로 "신이 내린 선물", "천국의 열매"가 아닌가.

BREAKFAST AT AL JAZEERA

Breakfast on the Al Jazeera Plains is simple but hearty. "After the first rain and seeing the first face, today is a good day. Brother from afar, let us break bread together." Lemon juice and pepper are sprinkled over sheep's milk yogurt, drizzled with fresh olive oil harvested this year, pickled plums and pickled pepper, herb cheese and wild honey, bread baked in an oven and shai are brought out. When the sharp and fresh fragrance of the olive oil that goes into every meal spreads throughout your mouth, olives are truly "gifts from God" and "fruits of Paradise."

Tell Beydar, Kurdistan, Syria, 2008.

날 마 다 소 풍

태양이 수직으로 작열하는 광야의 낮은 쉼의 시간.
이른 아침에 일을 하고 잠깐 낮잠을 자고 나서
삼삼오오 다과를 들고 올리브나무 숲으로 향한다.
새파란 하늘에 눈동자를 씻고
시원한 바람에 마음을 맑히고
다정한 담소를 나누는 느긋한 시간.
바람을 쏘이며 올리브나무 숲으로 가는
이 소풍逍風은 빼놓을 수 없는 일과이다.

DAILY PICNIC

Midday in the wilderness when the sun burns down vertically is a time for
rest. After working since early in the morning then taking a short nap, in twos
and threes people head for the olive grove, carrying snacks, a leisurely time
for washing eyes in the deep blue sky, letting the cool wind clear the mind, for
sharing a friendly chat. Refreshed by the breeze, heading for the olive grove,
this picnic is an indispensable daily routine.

Jerash, Jordan, 2008.

영혼을 위한 자리

알 자지라 평원에 자리한 소박한 농부의 집.
따스한 햇살이 감싸는 흙벽에 기대앉아
향기 진한 아라빅 커피를 마시며 깊은숨을 쉰다.
이토록 작은 영토, 작은 장소, 작은 올리브나무인데
왜 이리 넉넉하고 따스하고 아늑하여
그대와 함께 오래오래 앉아있고 싶은지.
작지만 오롯한, 영혼을 위한 자리 하나.

A PLACE FOR THE SOUL

A simple farmer's house on the plains of Al Jazeera. Leaning against
the earthen wall bathed in the warm sunlight, take a deep breath while
drinking fragrant Arabic coffee. Such a small territory, such a small space,
such a small olive tree, so content, warm and cozy, I long to sit here
with you for a long time. A small but full place for the soul.

Tell Mardikh, Syria, 2008.

저 녁 을 준 비 하 는 여 인

시리아 국경 사막지대의 삶은 고달프다.

여름에는 뜨거운 열풍이 땅을 가르고

겨울에는 추위가 뼛속까지 파고든다.

시리아 쿠르드인들은 언제 쫓겨날지 모를

불안한 삶의 무게까지 지고 살아야 한다.

황량한 사막에서 그이들을 지켜온 것은

마을 공터와 집 마당에 심겨진 올리브나무.

"풀 죽은 아이들에게 말해주곤 하지요.

올리브나무처럼 살아야 한다고요.

누가 돌봐주지 않아도 스스로 강인하고

자신을 아낌없이 내어주는 올리브나무처럼요.

하느님은 올리브나무를 택하여 우릴 지켜주고 있으니."

A WOMAN PREPARING DINNER

Life in the desert area on the Syrian border is hard. In summer,
a hot wind cuts through the land, in winter, the cold penetrates to the bone.
Syrian Kurds never know when they will be kicked out. They have to live with
the burden of an anxious life. What has kept them in the desolate wilderness
are the olive trees planted in the village's vacant lot and in the yard of the house.
"I often tell discouraged children: You have to live like an olive tree,
which is strong on its own and gives of itself generously,
even if no one takes care of it. God chose the olive tree to protect us."

Al Qamishli, Syria, 2008.

A YOUNG TREE IN THE WILDERNESS

A young olive tree along the desert road on the border between Iraq and Syria.
It was swaying as if about to collapse in a hot sandstorm. A tree starts a lonely fight
from the moment it is planted. It has to take root in a place it couldn't choose,
has to do its best to survive and stay green. People want to live comfortably,
want to live easily, but it seems that it is heaven's way to enable those whose
lives have been forged by strong sunlight and harsh winds to bear noble fruits.
We gain the strength to live again when we are moved and comforted
by such a tree, such a creation, such a person.

On the Way to Iraq from Palmyra, Syria, 2007.

사막의 어린 나무

이라크와 시리아 국경 사막 길의 어린 올리브나무.
뜨거운 모래 폭풍에 쓰러질 듯 흔들리고 있었다.
나무는 심긴 그 순간부터 외로운 싸움을 시작한다.
선택할 수 없는 이 자리에서 스스로 뿌리를 내리고
최선을 다해 살아남고 푸르러야만 한다.
사람은 편하게 살고 싶고, 쉽게 살기를 바라지만,
강한 불볕과 모진 바람으로 인생을 단련시킨 자에게
고귀한 열매를 맺게 하는 건 하늘의 방식인가 보다.
우리는 그런 나무, 그런 창조, 그런 사람에게
감동하고 위로받고 다시 살아갈 힘을 얻으니.

점령지의 푸른 띠

이곳은 예수가 태어난 베들레헴.
이스라엘에 점령당한 이 땅에서
팔레스타인 사람들은 예수 이전부터 대대로 일궈온
올리브 밭조차 자유롭게 출입할 수 없다.
허가증을 받은 약 20%의 농민만이
수확기에 단 며칠만 접근이 허가된다.
이스라엘이 늘려가는 창백한 도시 '정착촌'.
그 맞은편에 최후의 진을 치고 버티는 듯
올리브나무들이 푸른 띠를 잇고 서 있다.

A GREEN BELT IN THE OCCUPIED TERRITORIES

This is Bethlehem, where Jesus was born. In this land occupied by Israel
even the olive groves are not freely accessible to the Palestinians who have been
working here for generations, since before Jesus. Only about 20% of farmers,
those with permits, are granted access for just a few days during the harvest.
There are Israel's spreading pallid settlements and on the opposite side
as if they were making a last stand, olive trees form a green belt.

Bethlehem, Palestine, 2005.

"THIS WALL WILL COLLAPSE"

The greatest prison on earth, the separation barrier was built by Israel,
financed by the United States. However, this barrier is a prison that
isolates itself from the world, as high as the height of their sinful karma.
Standing tall alone in front of the huge separation barrier an olive tree
seems to be protesting with its whole body. "This wall will eventually collapse."
The olive tree of prophecy cries out with 'the voice of the wilderness.'

Bethlehem, Palestine, 2005.

"이 벽은 무너지리라"

지상의 가장 거대한 감옥, 분리장벽.
미국이 돈을 대고 이스라엘이 건축했다.
그러나 이 장벽은 자신들의 죄업의 높이만큼
세계로부터 스스로를 고립시키는 감옥이니.
거대한 분리장벽 앞에 홀로 우뚝 서서
온몸으로 시위하는 것만 같은 올리브나무.
"이 벽은 끝내 무너지고 말리라"
'광야의 목소리'로 외치는 예언의 올리브나무.

절망의 벽에 새긴 희망

장벽을 쌓고 철망을 쳐도 영혼은 가로막지 못한다.
세계 각지에서 찾아온 청년들과 예술가들은
이 시대 최악의 건축물인 이스라엘의 분리장벽을
저항과 해방의 화폭으로 바꿔놓았다.
"우리의 절망에서 희망의 불꽃이 솟구친다"는 문구 위로
둥치는 베어졌어도 나이테는 모든 것을 기억한다는 듯
올리브나무 벽화가 펼쳐지고, 희망의 노래는 계속된다.
자유롭게 살 수 없다면, 나무처럼 서서 죽으리!

HOPE ENGRAVED ON THE WALL
OF DESPAIR

Even if you build a barrier and set up barbed wire, the soul cannot be blocked.
Young people and artists from all over the world have turned Israel's
separation barrier, the worst building of our time into a canvas of resistance
and liberation. Above the phrase "Out of our hopelessness spring the flames
of our hope" as if tree rings remember everything even though the tree trunks
are cut down, the olive tree mural unfolds, and the song of hope continues.
If we can't live freely, we'll die standing like trees!

Bethlehem, Palestine, 2008.

목 잘린 천 년의 올리브나무

이스라엘이 팔레스타인 서안지구를 점령한
1967년 이후 최소 250만 그루의 올리브나무가
불태워지고, 목 잘리고, 뿌리 뽑혀 나갔다.
백 년도 살지 못하는 점령자의 손에 잘려나간
천 년의 올리브나무가 하늘을 향해 부르짖나니.
'모든 사람이 잊어버려도 내가 기억한다.
모든 사람이 침묵하여도 내가 증언한다.
모든 사람이 쓰러져가도 내가 여기 서 있다.'
천 년의 기억을 품고, 살아서나 죽어서나.

THOUSAND-YEAR-OLD OLIVE TREES DECAPITATED

Since 1967, when Israel occupied the Palestinian West Bank, at least 2.5 million olive trees have been burned, decapitated, and uprooted. Cut down by the hands of an occupant who hasn't even lived a hundred years, thousand-year-old olive trees cry out to the heavens. 'Even if everyone forgets, I remember. Even if everyone is silent, I testify. Even if everyone falls, I'm still standing here.' Embracing the memory of a thousand years, alive or dead.

Salfit, Palestine, 2008.

난민촌의 포스터

팔레스타인 난민촌에서는 나무를 찾아보기 어렵다.
나무를 심을 땅이 없기 때문이다.
이스라엘에 의해 뿌리 뽑힌 고향 땅의 올리브나무를
포스터에 담아 거리마다 붙여둔 난민들.
이 나무들처럼 뿌리 뽑혀 떠돌고 있는 난민들은
언젠가 자유의 대지에 심은 올리브나무 아래서
푸른 잎을 날리며 살아갈 그날만을 꿈꾼다.

REFUGEE CAMP POSTERS

Trees are hard to find in Palestinian refugee camps because there is nowhere
left to plant trees. The refugees have put up on posters in the streets the olive
trees of their native land uprooted by Israel. Refugees, uprooted and drifting
like those trees, only dream of the day when they will live with flying green
leaves under olive trees planted in a land of freedom.

'Ain Al-Hilweh' Palestine Refugee Camp, Saida, Lebanon, 2008.

천 년 의 시 작 은 이 렇 게

나무가 잘려나가고 좋은 땅을 빼앗겨도
팔레스타인 농부들은 황무지를 일구며
다시 어린 올리브나무를 심어나간다.
척박한 땅에서 올리브나무 하나 키우기란
아이를 기르듯 공력을 들여야 하는 일이다.
모래바람과 짐승들로부터 보호하기 위해
한 그루 한 그루 낡은 드럼통으로 감싸고
그 위에 팔레스타인 국기를 상징하는
초록, 하양, 빨강색을 기원하듯 칠해두었다.
이 작고 여린 나무들 중에 끝내 살아남아
다시 천 년을 이어갈 올리브나무가 있으리니.
그토록 길고 큰 '사랑의 나무'의 시작은
얼마나 미약하고 눈물겨운지.

A THOUSAND YEARS BEGINS LIKE THIS

Even if the trees are cut down and the good land is taken away,
Palestinian farmers plow barren land and plant young olive trees again.
Growing an olive tree in a barren land is something that requires effort,
just like raising a child. To protect them from sandstorms and animals,
enclosing each tree in an old drum painted green, white, and red to represent
the Palestinian flag, as if wishing. Among these small and fragile trees,
there will be an olive tree that will finally survive and last a thousand years.
How feeble and tearful, the beginning of such a long and large 'Tree of Love'.

Ramallah, Palestine, 2008.

예 수 가 태 어 난 자 리 에

예수가 태어난 구유 자리에 세워진 '예수 탄생 교회'.
세계에서 찾아오는 순례객들로 발 디딜 틈이 없다.
여러 종파의 각기 다른 십자가가 차지한 하늘 아래
한 그루의 올리브나무 고목이 묵연히 서 있다.
잘린 올리브나무에서 새순이 커나가고 있다.

THE PLACE WHERE JESUS WAS BORN

The 'Church of the Nativity' built on the site of the manger where Jesus was
born. No room for the pilgrims from all over the world to stand. Under the sky
occupied by different crosses of various denominations, a single old olive tree
stands silently. New shoots are growing from the cut olive tree.

Bethlehem, Palestine, 2005.

폭격 속에 살아남아

이스라엘은 2006년 레바논을 침공했다.
주변의 고층 건물은 다 파괴되었는데
폭격에 살아남은 올리브나무는
잿빛 먼지를 뒤집어쓴 채 새잎을 내고 있었다.
매일 폐허 더미를 헤치며 세간살이 하나라도
더 건져보려 애를 쓰는 여인들은
살아남은 이 나무를 '희망의 나무'라 불렀다.
이것도 희망이라고…. 그래, 이것이 희망이라고.

SURVIVAL AMIDST THE BOMBING

Israel invaded Lebanon in 2006. After all the high-rise buildings around it were destroyed, an olive tree that had survived the bombing, covered in gray dust, was putting out new leaves. Women who every day go through the piled-up ruins, trying to find more household items, even if only one, call this surviving tree the 'Tree of Hope'. Saying that this too is hope…. Yes, this is hope.

Dahieh, Beirut, Lebanon, 2006.

묘석 위의 올리브 가지

전쟁보다 더 무서운 것은 전쟁 그 후이다.
파괴는 한순간이지만 재건은 긴 가난과 노동이고,
죽은 자는 산 자의 가슴에서 매일 다시 죽는다.
살아남은 이들은 마을 묘지를 조성해
올리브나무 가지를 바치며 경전을 읽고 기도한다.
"죄 없이 죽은 자는 높은 자리에 있으리라."
신의 손길을 대신하듯 올리브나무 가지가
차가운 묘비를 푸른 숨결로 어루만진다.

AN OLIVE BRANCH ON A GRAVESTONE

What is scarier than war is what comes after war. Destruction is fleeting, but
reconstruction is long poverty and labor. The dead die every day in the hearts
of the living. Survivors set up village cemeteries, offering olive branches,
reading scriptures and praying. "Those who die without sin will be exalted."
The olive branches comfort the cold tombstones with their green breath
as if representing the hand of God.

Dahieh, Beirut, Lebanon, 2006.

NEW LEAVES SPROUT ON A BURNT TREE

Cana Village is recorded as the place where Jesus's first miracle was performed, turning water into wine at a wedding feast. A bomb dropped by Israel in 2006 killed 65 people, 35 of them children. 'You child who laughed beneath an olive tree, you fell asleep under an olive tree. Now you will never wake but you will awaken the sleeping world.' An olive tree that has sprouted new leaves from its burnt body stands indifferent, as if praying towards the blue sky.

Qana, Lebanon, 2006.

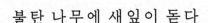

불탄 나무에 새잎이 돋다

예수가 혼인 잔치에서 물을 포도주로 바꾸는
첫 기적을 행한 곳으로 기록된 까나 마을.
2006년 이스라엘이 떨어트린 폭탄으로
65명이 사상했고 그중 35명이 아이들이었다.
'올리브나무 아래 웃음 짓던 아이야.
올리브나무 아래 잠이 들고 말았구나.
이제 너는 영영 깨어나지 않으리.
그러나 너는 잠든 세상을 깨우리.'
불탄 몸으로 새잎을 틔워낸 올리브나무가
무심히도 파란 하늘을 향해 기도하듯 서 있다.

나무와 함께 자란 소녀

시리아 평원의 흙집은 흙에서 태어나 흙을 일구고
다시 흙으로 돌아가는 이들의 순박한 일생과 닮았다.
거친 흙바람 속에서도 모든 것이 정갈하다.
아픈 엄마가 해온 것처럼 날마다 흙마당을 쓸고 닦고
올리브나무에 물을 주는 건 소녀의 몫이다.
엄마가 손수 만들어준 솜 인형을 안고 서 있는
소녀의 작은 몸에 긴 그림자가 드리워져 있는데….
하지만 소녀야, 그림자가 없는 곳은 어둠뿐이란다.
그림자는 빛을 품은 자의 숙명이란다.
슬픔도 아픔도 그림자처럼 동행하며
마음의 빛을 잃지 말고 자라나는 거란다.

THE GIRL WHO GREW UP WITH TREES

The earthen houses of the plains of Syria resemble the simple lives of those
who are born of earth, cultivate earth, then return to earth again. Even in
the rough dusty wind, everything is tidy. Sweeping, cleaning the dirt yard and
watering the olive tree every day, just like her sick mother did, are the girl's lot.
As she stands hugging a stuffed toy her mother made for her, a long shadow
is cast over the girl's small body…. But girl, the only place without a shadow is
darkness. Shadows are the fate of those who embrace the light. Accompanied
by sorrow and pain like shadows, grow up never losing the heart's light.

Tell Beydar, Syria, 2008.

고원의 격려자

분쟁터를 누비다 나도 많이 다쳤다.

전쟁의 세상에서 내 안에 전쟁이 들어서려 할 때,

다친 몸을 이끌고 올리브나무 아래로 간다.

저 높은 고원에 나를 마중 나오신 듯한 나무 하나.

몸을 기울여 오래오래 기다려오신 듯한 나무 하나.

나는 그만 올리브나무에 기대앉아 아이처럼 운다.

눈물 속에 한순간 잠이 들고나면, 그러면,

내 안에 빛과 힘이 차오르고, 다시 나의 길을 간다.

말 없는 격려, 속 깊은 사랑, 은밀한 가호.

언제나 그 자리에 서서 나를 기다리고 지켜주는 나무 하나.

세상에는 그토록 묵중하고 한결같은 사랑의 사람 하나 있다.

HIGHLAND ENCOURAGER

I too was badly hurt while crossing battlefields. When war is about to enter me
in this world full of war, I steer my injured body beneath an olive tree, a tree
that seems to be greeting me on that high plateau, a tree that seems to have been
waiting for a long time, leaning over. I stay leaning against the olive tree and weep
like a child. If I fall asleep for a moment in tears, then, light and strength fill me
and I set off on my way again. Silent encouragement, deep love, secret protection.
A tree that always stands there waiting for me and protecting me.
There is one person of love in this world who is so profound and unfailing.

Jerash, Jordan, 2008.

십 자 가 는 부 러 져 도

모래바람에 녹슬어 부러진 십자가는
그냥 지나가지 않는 세월의 무게를 전하는데.
가릴 것 하나 없는 불타는 광야에 심겨진
작은 올리브나무들은 오늘도 푸르게 자란다.
올리브나무는 땅속의 뿌리 하나하나가
지상의 가지와 핏줄처럼 이어져 있어,
실뿌리 하나라도 물기를 찾으면 온 힘으로
자양을 빨아올리며 그 오랜 세월을 살아낸다.
자신의 자리에 한 번 뿌리내린 올리브나무는
아무리 작아도 시간이 희망이다.

EVEN IF THE CROSS IS BROKEN

The cross has rusted and broken in sandstorms. It conveys the weight of
the years that don't just pass. Planted in the burning wilderness with nothing
to shade them, small olive trees grow green today. The olive tree's roots
underground are all connected like veins to the branches above the ground.
If even one little root finds moisture, it will use all its strength to suck up
nourishment and survive for long years. For an olive tree once rooted in
its place, no matter how small, time is hope.

The Wilderness East of Bethlehem, Palestine, 2005.

석 양 의 기 도

알 자지라 신화에서 창세기로 전해진 '노아의 방주' 이야기.
노아는 비둘기가 올리브 새잎을 물고 오는 것을 보고
홍수의 시대는 끝났으며 새로운 삶을 시작할 때임을 알았다.
이로부터 올리브 가지를 문 비둘기는 평화의 상징이 되었다.
전란의 땅에 노을이 물들고 오늘도 긴 아잔 소리가 울릴 때
하루 일을 마친 농부는 올리브나무 사이에서 기도를 바친다.
파괴된 대지에 가장 먼저 피어났던 저 올리브 새싹처럼,
사무치는 마음으로 삶에 대한 감사를 드린다.

SUNSET PRAYER

The story of 'Noah's Ark,' passed down from Al Jazeera myth to Genesis.
Noah saw the dove carrying a young olive leaf. He realized that the era of
the flood was over and it was time to start a new life. Since then, the dove
bearing an olive branch has become a symbol of peace. When the sunset colors
the land of war and the long sound of Azan resounds again, after his day's work,
the farmer prays among the olive trees. Like that olive sprout that first bloomed
on the devastated land, giving thanks for life with a poignant heart.

Tell Mardikh, Syria, 2008.

BENEATH AN OLIVE TREE

Children tending sheep read a book beneath an olive tree. On the day they had
their first outing, their first day at school, the day they confessed their first love,
on the day they promised a friend who was fleeing that they must live and meet again,
even on the day they bade farewell to a brother who died in battle, they cried,
laughed and prayed beneath this tree. Likewise the children's mothers and fathers,
grandmothers and grandfathers. In this land, everything begins beneath an olive tree.
Important events in life that begin, something noble decided, the layers of memories
and inner rings I have grown up with are engraved. A spotlight shining
on the destination of my life, one tree is a unique place.

Hebron, Palestine, 2008.

올리브나무 아래

양을 치던 아이들이 올리브나무 아래 책을 읽는다.
첫 나들이 하던 날도, 첫 등교 날도, 첫사랑을 고백한 날도,
피난 가는 친구에게 우리 꼭 살아서 다시 만나자 언약한 날도,
전사한 형을 떠나보낸 날도, 이 나무 아래 울고 웃고 기도했다.
아이들의 엄마와 아빠도, 할머니와 할아버지도 그러했다.
이 땅에서는 올리브나무 아래 모든 일이 시작된다.
삶의 중요한 사건이 탄생하고, 고귀한 무언가가 맺어지고,
내가 성장해온 기억의 층들과 내면의 나이테가 새겨진다.
내 인생의 목적지를 비춰주는 한 점 빛의 자리.
한 그루의 나무는, 하나의 유일무이한 장소이다.

나의 나무는

광야의 마을 길에서 만난 열두 살 마흐무드에게
네가 가진 가장 소중한 게 뭐냐고 물었다.
소년은 올리브나무에 기대며 씨익 웃어 보인다.
"제가 맨 처음 타고 올라갔던 나무예요.
이 나무 아래서 놀고 일하다가 숙제도 해요.
제가 잘못하고 부끄러운 날에는요,
이 나무에 속삭이며 기대 울기도 해요.
저도 이 올리브나무처럼 단단하게 자라서
누군가에게 힘이 되는 사람이 되고 싶어요."
멀리서 불어오는 바람결에 올리브 잎은 휘날리고
소년에게서 나무의 숨결과 향기가 배어 나왔다.

MY TREE

I asked 12-year-old Mahmud, whom I met on a road in a village in
the wilderness, what was the most precious thing he had. The boy smiles
as he leans against an olive tree. "This is the first tree I ever climbed.
I play and work beneath this tree and do my homework. On the days when
I'm wrong and I'm ashamed, I whisper to this tree and lean on it and cry.
I want to grow up as strong as this olive tree, to be a person who can help
someone." The olive leaves fluttered in the wind blowing from far away,
the breath and scent of the tree flowed from the boy.

Jerash, Jordan, 2008.

나무는 나무를 부른다

나무는 언제나 처음에는 혼자다.
홀로 선 나무에 꽃이 피고 결실이 맺고
씨알이 떨어져 아주 작은 나무들이 자라고,
한 걸음 두 걸음 푸른 걸음마를 시작하면,
나무는 나무를 부른다. 숲은 숲을 부른다.
오랜 기억과 투혼을 이어받은 후대가
힘차게 자라나는 땅에서, 희망은 불멸이다.
그가 앞서 걸어온 수백 년의 걸음 따라
100년, 30년, 어린 나무들이 푸르게 빛난다.

TREE CALLS TO TREE

A tree is always alone at first. Flowers bloom and bear fruit on the tree
standing alone. The seeds fall and grow into very small trees, one step,
two steps, when the green baby steps begin, tree calls to tree, forest calls to forest.
In a land where descendants inheriting long memories and a fighting spirit
grow vigorously, hope is immortal. Following the hundreds of years it has gone
walking ahead 100 years, 30 years, young trees shine green.

Jerash, Jordan, 2008.

TAKE THIS FRUIT

When the small, light yellow flowers bloom and wither,
olives finally form. The fruit, their 'olive green' hue the best, unique
among green colors, become daily bread, noble oil, fragrant oil in
the sanctuary. An olive tree never loses its green color, from birth
until the day it dies. As if that was their mission. May the olive tree,
having endured all the trials of the sun and wind, say, 'My love
has been ripe for a long time. You, take this fruit and eat it.
Then, give the world taste and shine light on it.'

On the Way to Iraq from Palmyra, Syria, 2007.

이 열매를 받으라

작은 연노랑 꽃이 피고 지면 드디어 올리브 알들이 맺힌다.
초록 빛깔 중에서도 더없이 독특한 '올리브그린' 빛의 열매는
일용할 양식이 되고 고귀한 기름이 되고 성전의 향유가 된다.
올리브나무는 태어나서 죽는 날까지 푸른빛을 잃지 않는다.
그것이 자신의 사명이라는 듯이.
저 불볕과 바람의 시련을 다 받아낸 올리브나무가 이르길,
'내 사랑은 오래 익어왔다. 그대여 이 열매를 받아먹으라.
그리고, 세상에 맛을 내고 빛을 밝히라.'

믿음의 파수꾼처럼

뜨거운 광야의 태양이 천천히 기울고
지상의 모든 것이 붉게 물들어가면
귀가하는 양떼들의 방울소리와 함께
사원의 아잔 소리가 길게 울린다.
'고단했던 하루에 눈물짓는 사람아.
오늘의 노여움도 괴로움도
지는 해와 함께 보내주기를.
다시 아침이 밝아올 것이고
내일은 또 새로운 날이 시작될 것이니.
오늘 밤은 광야처럼 깊이 잠들기를.'
파수꾼처럼, 믿음의 파수꾼처럼 밤을 새워
나를 지켜주고 서 있는 천 년의 올리브나무.

LIKE A FAITHFUL WATCHMAN

The hot wilderness sun slowly sinks and when everything on the ground
turns red, with the tinkling of the bells of sheep returning home,
the mosque's Azan sounds long. 'You who shed tears on a tiring day,
let go of today's anger and suffering with the setting sun.
The morning will come again, tomorrow will begin another new day.
Tonight, I wish you a sleep deep like the wilderness.'
Staying awake all night like a watchman, like a faithful watchman,
a thousand-year-old olive tree stands and protects me.

Jerash, Jordan, 2008.

HOLDING A LAMB IN HIS ARMS

The boy who has sought and is carrying a lost lamb pauses for a moment
beneath an olive tree between the vast horizon and the boundless sky.
Wrapped in a dark blue light that seems to shine from eternity, time to ponder,
sensing the divinity dwelling in little me. That olive tree seems to be a secret
passage of light that connects heaven and earth, a lifetime and eternity.
In our lives, the 'passage of light' opens just as suddenly to everyone.
When you walk following the light, the path to the true self becomes brighter.
In times like these, the way we really contribute to the world would be
nothing else, but surely seeking my true self, loving and giving and living.
After leaning against the olive tree to catch his breath,
holding the lamb again, the boy slowly walks along the path as the stars rise.

Jerash, Jordan, 2008.

어린 양을 품에 안고

낙오된 어린 양을 찾아 안고 오던 소년은
막막한 지평과 가이없는 하늘 사이,
올리브나무 아래 잠시 걸음을 멈춘다.
영원에서 비춰오는 듯한 검푸른 빛에 감싸여
작은 내 안에 깃든 신성을 느끼며 침잠하는 시간.
저 올리브나무는 하늘과 땅을, 한 생과 영원을
이어주는 비밀스런 빛의 통로인 것만 같다.
우리 인생에는 누구에게나 불현듯 그 '빛의 통로'가 열린다.
그 빛을 따라 걸을 때 진정한 나에게 이르는 길이 밝아온다.
이런 시대에, 우리가 정말로 세상에 기여하는 길은
다른 무엇도 아닌 진정한 나 자신을 찾아가며
더 사랑하고 내어주며 살아가는 것이 아니겠는가.
올리브나무에 기대어 숨을 고르던 소년이
다시 양을 안고 천천히 별이 뜨는 길을 걸어간다.

전쟁의 레바논에서, 박노해. Park Nohae in the battlefield of Lebanon, 2007.

박노해

1957 전라남도에서 태어났다. 16세에 상경해 낮에는 노동자로 일하고 밤에는 선린상고(야간)를 다녔다. **1984** 27살에 첫 시집 『노동의 새벽』을 펴냈다. 이 시집은 독재 정권의 금서 조치에도 100만 부 가까이 발간되며 한국 사회와 문단을 충격으로 뒤흔들었다. 감시를 피해 사용한 박노해라는 필명은 '박해받는 노동자 해방'이라는 뜻으로, 이때부터 '얼굴 없는 시인'으로 알려졌다. **1989** 〈남한사회주의노동자동맹〉(사노맹)을 결성했다. **1991** 7년여의 수배 끝에 안기부에 체포, 24일간의 고문 후 '반국가단체 수괴' 죄목으로 사형이 구형되고 무기징역에 처해졌다. **1993** 감옥 독방에서 두 번째 시집 『참된 시작』을 펴냈다. **1997** 옥중에세이 『사람만이 희망이다』를 펴냈다. **1998** 7년 6개월 만에 석방되었다. 이후 민주화운동 유공자로 복권됐으나 국가보상금을 거부했다. **2000** "과거를 팔아 오늘을 살지 않겠다"며 권력의 길을 뒤로 하고 비영리단체 〈나눔문화〉(www.nanum.com)를 설립했다. **2003** 이라크 전쟁터에 뛰어들면서, 전 세계 가난과 분쟁의 현장에서 평화활동을 이어왔다. **2006** 레바논 내 세계 최대의 팔레스타인 난민촌 '아인 알 할웨'에 〈자이투나(올리브) 나눔문화학교〉를 설립, 18년째 지원을 이어가고 있다. **2010** 낡은 흑백 필름 카메라로 기록한 사진을 모아 첫 사진전 「라 광야」展과 「나 거기에 그들처럼」展(세종문화회관)을 열었다. 12년 만의 시집 『그러니 그대 사라지지 말아라』를 펴냈다. **2012** 나눔문화가 운영하는 〈라 카페 갤러리〉에서 상설 사진전을 개최, 22번의 전시 동안 38만 명이 관람했다. **2014** 사진전 「다른 길」展(세종문화회관) 개최와 함께 『다른 길』을 펴냈다. **2020** 첫 번째 시 그림책 『푸른 빛의 소녀가』를 펴냈다. **2021** 『걷는 독서』를 펴냈다. **2022** 12년 만의 시집 『너의 하늘을 보아』를 펴냈다. 30여 년간 써온 한 권의 책, '우주에서의 인간의 길'을 담은 사상서를 집필 중이다. '적은 소유로 기품 있게' 살아가는 〈참사람의 숲〉을 꿈꾸며, 시인의 작은 정원에서 꽃과 나무를 기르며 새로운 혁명의 길로 나아가고 있다.

매일, 사진과 글로 시작하는 하루 〈박노해의 걷는 독서〉 ⓘ park_nohae 🅕 parknohae

Park Nohae

He is a legendary poet, photographer and revolutionary. He was born in 1957. While working as a laborer in his 20s, he began to reflect and write poems on the sufferings of the laboring class. He then took the pseudonym Park Nohae("No" means "laborers," "Hae" means "liberation"). At the age of twenty-seven, Park published his first collection of poems, titled *Dawn of Labor*, in 1984. Despite official bans, this collection sold nearly a million copies, and it shook Korean society with its shocking emotional power. Since then, he became an intensely symbolic figure of resistance, often called the "Faceless Poet." For several years the government authorities tried to arrest him in vain. He was finally arrested in 1991. After twenty-four days of investigation, with illegal torture, the death penalty was demanded for his radical ideology. He was finally sentenced to life imprisonment. After seven and a half years in prison, he was pardoned in 1998. Thereafter, he was reinstated as a contributor to the democratization movement, but he refused any state compensation. Park decided to leave the way for power, saying, "I will not live today by selling the past," and he established a nonprofit social movement organization "Nanum Munhwa," meaning "Culture of Sharing,"(www.nanum.com) faced with the great challenges confronting global humanity. In 2003, right after the United States' invasion of Iraq, he flew to the field of war. Since then, he often visits countries that are suffering from war and poverty in order to raise awareness about the situation through his photos and writings. In 2006, he established 〈Zaituna(Olive) Nanum Munhwa School〉 in Ain Al-Hilweh, the world's largest Palestinian refugee camp in Lebanon, and he has been supporting the school for 18 years. He continues to hold photo exhibitions, and a total of 380,000 visitors have so far visited his exhibitions. He is writing a book of reflexions, the only such book he has written during the thirty years since prison, "The Human Path in Space." Dreaming of the Forest of True People, a life-community living "a graceful life with few possessions," the poet is still planting and growing flowers and trees in his small garden, advancing along the path toward a new revolution.

〈Park Nohae's Reading While Walking Along〉 ⓞpark_nohae ⨍parknohae

저서   Books

박노해 사진에세이 시리즈

01 하루 02 단순하게 단단하게 단아하게
03 길 04 내 작은 방 05 아이들은 놀라워라

박노해 시인이 20여 년 동안 지상의
멀고 높은 길을 걸으며 기록해온
'유랑노트'이자 길 찾는 이에게 띄우는
두꺼운 편지. 각 권마다 37점의 흑백
사진과 캡션이 담겼다. 인생이란 한 편
의 이야기이며 '에세이'란 그 이야기를
남기는 것이니. 삶의 화두와도 같은
주제로 해마다 새 시리즈가 출간된다.

136p | 20,000KRW | 2019-2022

Park Nohae Photo Essay

01 One Day 02 Simply, Firmly, Gracefully
03 The Path 04 My Dear Little Room
05 Children Are Amazing

These are 'wandering notes' that the
poet Park Nohae has recorded while
walking along the Earth's long, high roads
for over twenty years, a thick letter to
those who seek for a path. Each volume
contains 37 black-and-white photos
and captions. Life is a story, and each of
these 'essays' is designed to leave that
story behind. A new volume is published
every year like a topic of life.

너의 하늘을 보아

12년만의 신작 시집. 무언가 잘못된
세상에 절망할 때, 하루하루 내 영혼이
희미해져갈 때, 빛과 힘이 되어줄 301편의
시. 고난과 어둠 속에서도 '빛을 찾아가는
여정'에 자신을 두었던 박노해 시인의
투혼과 사랑의 삶이 전하는 울림. 그 시를
읽기 전의 나로 돌아갈 수 없는 강렬한
체험."아무것도 없다고 생각되는 순간
조차, 우리에게는 자신만의 하늘이 있다."

528p | 19,500KRW | 2022

Seeing Your Heaven

A new collection of poems, the first in 12 years.
301 poems that will give you light and strength
when you despair in a world gone wrong,
when your soul seems to be fading away
day by day. The reverberations of the life of
love and fighting spirit of poet Park Nohae,
who set out on a 'journey in search of light'
in the midst of hardship and darkness.
An intense experience that makes it impossible
to return to who I was before I read the poems.
"Even when we think there is nothing,
we each have our own heaven."

걷는 독서

단 한 줄로도 충분하다! 한 권의 책이
응축된 듯한 423편의 문장들. 박노해
시인이 감옥 독방에 갇혀서도, 국경 너머
분쟁 현장에서도 멈추지 않은 일생의
의례이자 창조의 원천인 '걷는 독서'.
온몸으로 살고 사랑하고 저항해온 삶의
정수가 담긴 문장과 세계의 숨은 빛을
담은 컬러사진이 어우러져 언제 어디를
펼쳐봐도 지혜와 영감이 깃든다.

880p | 23,000KRW | 2021

Reading While Walking Along

One line is enough! 423 sentences, one whole
book condensed into each sentence. 'Reading
While Walking Along' is a lifelong ritual and
source of creation by Park Nohae who never
stopped, even after being confined in solitary
confinement in a prison cell or at the scene of
conflicts beyond the border. The aphorisms that
contain the essence of his life, in which he has
lived, loved and resisted with his whole body,
are harmonized with color photos that contain
the hidden light of the world, delivering wisdom
and inspiration wherever we open them.

푸른 빛의 소녀가

박노해 시인의 첫 번째 시 그림책. 저 먼 행성에서 찾아온 푸른 빛의 소녀와 지구별 시인의 가슴 시린 이야기. "지구에서 좋은 게 뭐죠?" 우주적 시야로 바라본 삶의 근본 물음과 아이들의 가슴에 푸른 빛의 상상력을 불어넣는 신비로운 여정이 펼쳐진다. "우리 모두는 별에서 온 아이들. 네 안에는 별이 빛나고 있어."(박노해)

72p | 19,500KRW | 2020

The Blue Light Girl

Poet Park Nohae's first Poetry Picture Book. The poignant tale of the Blue Light Girl visiting from a distant planet and a poet of Planet Earth. "What is good on Earth?" The fundamental question of life seen from a cosmic perspective. A mysterious journey inspiring an imagination of blue light in the heart of the children. "We are all children from the stars. Stars are shining in you."(Park Nohae)

다른 길

"우리 인생에는 각자가 진짜로 원하는 무언가가 있다. 분명, 나만의 다른 길이 있다." 인디아에서 파키스탄, 라오스, 버마, 인도네시아, 티베트까지 지도에도 없는 마을로 떠나는 여행. 그리고 그 길의 끝에서 진정한 나를 만나는 새로운 여행에세이. '이야기가 있는 사진'이 한 걸음 다른 길로 우리를 안내한다.

352p | 19,500KRW | 2014

Another Way

"In our lives, there is something which each of us really wants. For me, certainly, I have my own way, different from others"(Park Nohae). From India, Pakistan, Laos, Burma, Indonesia to Tibet, a journey to villages nowhere to be seen on the map. And a new essay of meeting true self at the end of the road. 'Image with a story' guide us to another way.

그러니 그대 사라지지 말아라

영혼을 뒤흔드는 시의 정수. 저항과 영성, 교육과 살림, 아름다움과 혁명 그리고 사랑까지 붉디 붉은 304편의 시가 담겼다. 인생의 갈림길에서 길을 잃고 헤매는 순간마다 어디를 펼쳐 읽어도 좋을 책. 입소문만으로 이 시집을 구입한 6만 명의 독자가 증명하는 감동. "그러니 그대 사라지지 말아라" 그 한 마디가 나를 다시 살게 한다.

560p | 18,000KRW | 2010

So You Must Not Disappear

The essence of soul-shaking poetry! This anthology of 304 poems as red as its book cover, narrating resistance, spiri- tuality, education, living, the beautiful, revolution and love. Whenever you're lost at a crossroads of your life, it will guide you with any page of it moving you. The intensity of moving is evidenced by the 60,000 readers who have bought this book only through word-of-mouth. "So you must not disappear." This one phrase makes me live again.

노동의 새벽

1984년, 27살의 '얼굴 없는 시인'이 쓴 시집 한 권이 세상을 뒤흔들었다. 독재 정부의 금서 조치에도 100만 부 이상 발간되며 화인처럼 새겨진 불멸의 고전. 억압받는 천만 노동자의 영혼의 북소리로 울려퍼진 노래. "박노해는 역사이고 상징이며 신화다. 문학사적으로나 사회사적으로 우리는 그런 존재를 다시 만날 수 없을지 모른다."(문학평론가 도정일)

172p | 12,000KRW | 2014
30th Anniversary Edition

Dawn of Labor

In 1984, an anthology of poems written by 27 years old 'faceless poet' shook Kor- ean society. Recorded as a million seller despite the publication ban under military dictatorship, it became an immortal classic ingrained like a marking iron. It was a song echoing down with the throbbing pulses of ten million workers' souls. "Park Nohae is a history, a symbol, and a myth. All the way through the history of literature and society alike, we may never meet such a being again."(Doh Jeong-il, literary critic)

올리브나무 아래

박노해 사진에세이 06

2판 3쇄 발행 2024년 1월 3일
초판 1쇄 발행 2023년 9월 25일

사진·글 박노해
번역 안선재
편집 김예슬, 윤지영
표지 디자인 홍동원
자문 이기명 아날로그 인화 유철수
보정 신상윤 제작 윤지혜
홍보 마케팅 이상훈 인쇄 천광인쇄사
제본 광성문화사 후가공 신화사금박

발행인 임소희
발행처 느린걸음
출판등록 2002년 3월 15일 제300-2009-109호
주소 서울시 종로구 사직로8길 34, 330호
전화 02-733-3773
팩스 02-734-1976
이메일 slow-walk@slow-walk.com
홈페이지 www.slow-walk.com
instagram.com/slow_walk_book

ISBN 978-89-91418-35-6 04810
ISBN 978-89-91418-25-7 04810(세트)

번역자 안선재(안토니 수사)는 서강대학교 명예교수로
50권 이상의 한국 시와 소설의 영문 번역서를 펴냈다.

Beneath the Olive Tree

Park Nohae Photo Essay 06

Second edition, third publishing, Jan. 3, 2024
First edition, first publishing, Sep. 25, 2023

Photographed and Written by Park Nohae
Translated by Brother Anthony of Taizé
Edited by Kim Yeseul, Yun Jiyoung
Cover Designed by Hong Dongwon
Consulted by Lee Ki-Myoung
Photographic Analogue Prints by Yu Chulsu
Production by Yun Jihye
Photo Retouching by Shin Sangyoon
Marketing by Lee Sanghoon

Publisher Im Sohee
Publishing Company Slow Walking
Address Rm330, 34, Sajik-ro 8-gil, Jongno-gu,
Seoul, Republic of Korea
Tel 82-2-7333773 Fax 82-2-7341976
E-mail slow-walk@slow-walk.com
Website www.slow-walk.com
instagram.com/slow_walk_book

ISBN 978-89-91418-35-6 04810
ISBN 978-89-91418-25-7 04810(SET)

Translator An Sonjae(Brother Anthony of Taizé)
is professor emeritus at Sogang University.
He has published over fifty volumes of
translations of Korean poetry and fiction.